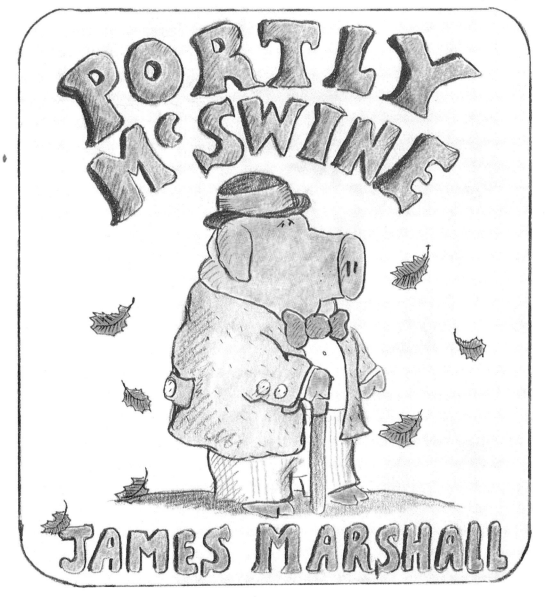

PORTLY McSWINE

JAMES MARSHALL

Houghton Mifflin Company Boston

www.houghtonmifflinbooks.com

Library of Congress Cataloging-in-Publication Data
Marshall, James, 1942–1992.
Portly McSwine.
Summary: Despite all attempts to reassure him, Portly McSwine
frets about the National Snout Day celebration he has planned.
[1. Pigs—Fiction. 2. Parties—Fiction.] I. Title.
PZ7.M35672Po [E] 78-24814
RNF ISBN 0-618-18381-7   PAP ISBN 0-618-18380-9

Printed in Singapore
TWP 10 9 8 7 6 5 4 3 2 1

For Adolph Garza
and
Modesto Torre

Portly McSwine gazed out the window. National Snout Day was only a day away, and Portly was planning a huge party. "Oh dear," he said. "I've never given a party before."

At his office McSwine couldn't concentrate
on his work.

"Stop worrying," said Esther his secretary.
"You'll make yourself sick."

After work Portly had a troubling thought.
"Oh my," he said. "What if I should get sick?"
He imagined how disappointed his party
guests would be.

Portly decided to stop at the
doctor's for a flu shot.
"Quit fretting," said the doctor.
"I'm sure your party will be
very amusing."

Outside the doctor's Portly stopped short.
"Oh golly," he said. "What if my party isn't
amusing enough?"
He imagined his guests groaning with
boredom.

People on the street couldn't help noticing
that Portly was talking to himself.
He was rehearsing his most amusing stories
to tell at the party.

In front of the fudge shop Portly
ran into his old friend Emily Pig.
"Will there be refreshments at the
party?" asked Emily.
"But of course," said Portly.

Stopping for a rest, Portly had a
disturbing idea.
"Oh gracious," he said. "What if my
refreshments aren't tasty enough?"
He imagined his guests all hopping
mad and complaining.

Portly decided to stop at the baker's. "I want to make sure my refreshments are the tastiest in town," he said. "Quit fussing," said the lady behind the counter.

A block from home Portly ran into
Emily again.
"Will there be dancing at the party?"
asked Emily.
"Certainly," replied Portly.

That night Portly had difficulty sleeping.
"Oh, oh," he said. "What if my dancing
isn't up to snuff?"
He could imagine his guests all *screaming*
with laughter.

Portly jumped out of bed and turned
on his gramophone.
He practiced waltzing around the living
room until he was sure his dancing was
perfectly fine.

The next day Portly's palms began to sweat.
"My party is *tonight*!" he gasped.
"Stop upsetting yourself," said Esther his
secretary. "I'm sure *everyone* will have a
wonderful time."

Portly went home, put up the party
decorations, put on his fancy
party clothes, and sat down to wait.
"What if *no* one comes?" he said.
Just then the doorbell rang.

All the guests arrived at once.
"Party time!" they shouted. And they
headed for the refreshment table.

"The French pastry is delicious!"
squealed Emily.
"This is the best National Snout
Day party *ever*!" cried another guest.
Everyone seemed to be having a
wonderful time.

Portly danced with Esther.
"You see," said Esther, "there was
nothing to worry about. I can
hardly wait until next year's party."

The following day Portly McSwine gazed
out the window.
National Snout Day was only three hundred
and sixty-four days away, and Portly was
planning a huge party.
"Oh dear," he said. "What if next year's
party isn't so good as this year's? Oh dear,
oh dear."